THIS WALKER BOOK BELONGS TO:

_____

_____

_____

_____

To little ghouls
everywhere,
especially
Finbar and Sally

First published 1993 by
Walker Books Ltd
87 Vauxhall Walk, London SE11 5HJ

This edition published 2000

2 4 6 8 10 9 7 5 3

© 1993 Colin and Jacqui Hawkins

This book has been typeset in Bernhard.

Printed in Hong Kong

British Library Cataloguing in Publication Data
A catalogue record for this book is
available from the British Library.

ISBN 0-7445-7794-2

Come for a Ride on the
GHOST TRAIN

Colin & Jacqui
Hawkins

WALKER BOOKS
AND SUBSIDIARIES
LONDON · BOSTON · SYDNEY

Come for a ride

on the Ghost Train.

In the dark dark

Over the loath—

some pit you will...

SSHRIEEK!

Out in the slimy

swamp you will...

Deep in the scary

forest you will...

In the gruesome

graveyard you will...

At the haunted

chapel you will…

In the dark dark

crypt you will...

In the creepy casket, in the

dark dark crypt you will find...

Come for a Ride on the Ghost Train

COLIN AND JACQUI HAWKINS have had an enthusiastic (and loud) response to *Come for a Ride on the Ghost Train*. They say, "It's a real favourite – probably one of the best reader/listener participation books we have provided. Without fail, when read to any group of children, they will, with enormously voluble gusto, sscream! sshriek! and ssqueeal! at each turn of the page. Great fun for all concerned – the noise can be off the decibel scale! (Readers might like to use cotton-wool ear plugs.)"

Jacqui Hawkins was born in Oxford in 1945. She attended Goldsmiths College before joining a design studio where she worked on exhibition and graphic design. Colin was born in Blackpool, also in 1945, and attended Blackpool College of Art. He then worked in the design department of the *Daily Express* for a number of years.

Colin and Jacqui began working together when their son was a baby, and have never looked back. They are now one of the most prolific and successful author/illustrator partnerships in the world of children's books. They have achieved particular acclaim for their inventive "novelty" books, including the Fingerwiggles series. Their other picture books for Walker include *Terrible, Terrible Tiger*, *The Wizard's Cat* and *Where's My Mummy?*. They live in Blackheath in London.

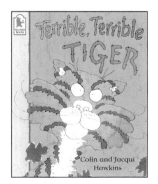

ISBN 0-7445-5230-3 (pb)

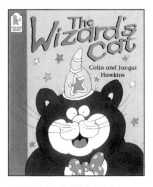

ISBN 0-7445-5231-1 (pb)

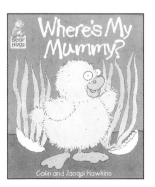

ISBN 0-7445-3041-5 (pb)

ISBN 0-7445-4491-2 (hb)